Lupita's Quincinera

Lupita's Quincinera

A Celebration to Remember

Shirley A. Franklin

iUniverse, Inc.
New York Bloomington

Lupita's Quincinera
A Celebration to Remember

Copyright © 2008 by Shirley A. Franklin

This is a work of fiction. All of the characters, names, incidents, organizations, and dialogue in this novel are either the products of the author's imagination or are used fictitiously.

iUniverse books may be ordered through booksellers or by contacting:

iUniverse
1663 Liberty Drive
Bloomington, IN 47403
www.iuniverse.com
1-800-Authors (1-800-288-4677)

Because of the dynamic nature of the Internet, any Web addresses or links contained in this book may have changed since publication and may no longer be valid. The views expressed in this work are solely those of the author and do not necessarily reflect the views of the publisher, and the publisher hereby disclaims any responsibility for them.

ISBN: 978-1-4401-0234-9 (pbk)
ISBN: 978-1-4401-0235-6 (ebk)

iUniverse rev. date: 11/18/08

Printed in the United States of America

"Padrina, you look amazing, just beautiful," Lupita gushed as she stepped back to let her godmother into THE GOOD HOUSE.

Dressed in a radish red pant suit, Lupita's godmother twirled around the foyer to show off her 100-pound lighter figure. Gabriela had stayed away for a few months so they wouldn't see her until her transformation was complete. She hugged Lupita, who was also her niece.

Lupita's parents joined in the praise. Pablo Fuentes was proud of his sister and overflowing with happiness at seeing her wear a genuine smile unlike any he'd seen in a while. Shy, reserved Maria Fuentes waited quietly and then embraced her sister-in-law and ushered her into the living room where a tray of raw vegetables and hummus, a Greek dip, was set out for all to enjoy.

As they all sat around the coffee table snacking, Lupita felt goose bumps running through her chubby body. She had tried the vegetables with hummus dip, but the new taste challenged her taste buds too much. It was from a recipe her papa had gotten from his Greek boss. Besides, she was about to burst with her own news.

Tia Gabriela tossed her head to remove her dark mane from her face. She nibbled on a celery stalk and between bites she explained how her Lap Band surgery had narrowed her stomach and allowed her to get fuller faster when eating. Everybody knew it had been her last resort after years of dieting with little or no results.

"It just doesn't take as much food for me to feel satisfied," she said as she waved her hand above the tray. She sat back and let everyone else enjoy the appetizers while Lupita's mom went to check on the stove-top enchiladas bubbling away in the kitchen. "And I do a lot of walking and drink lots of distilled water," she concluded.

Later at the table, Tia Gabriela sipped a glass of water. Her eyes danced in merriment when she looked at her niece.

Lupita sat up in her chair, placed her hands palm down on the table and got it out of her system. "I'm having Lap Band surgery in two months." "I'll look so much better during my Quince Anos. She explained - "All the girls in my court are smaller than me." In a quieter voice she added, "A lot smaller than me."

Everyone waited for the news to sink in. Parental eyes volleyed back and forth from Lupita to Gabriela like they were having a tennis match. Lupita wanted her godmother's approval very much. Finally, above the drinking glass, Tia Gabriela's eyes began to twinkle. Lupita let out her breath. She knew what that meant.

The words that followed verified this. "Great, meja, you'll be so much healthier and happier." Lupita was awash with joy. She jumped up and ran around the table to hug her aunt.

Soon talk turned to the preparations, which would be largely coordinated by Lupita's mom and aunt. Lupita's tia drew out the next words "You know Lupita, I might have to trade in the Last Doll I've picked out for you." Although there was an air of mystery to her suggestion, Lupita didn't ask any questions. But she didn't want to put her aunt through any extra trouble.

"Tia, I am sure whatever you've chosen will be great." She smiled at her aunt as she drank her soda. While sipping, she eyed her aunt over her glass. Twinkling eye met twinkling eye! Lupita felt especially encouraged.

In the past, when Lupita got scolded at the dinner table, her aunt had remained silent. But she'd lift the glass of whatever she was drinking and the spark of light in her eyes let Lupita know that she had someone silently on her side. "It's okay, angel," the eyes seemed to say when Lupita's mom or dad would ask her to cut back on her food portions.

After dinner, Lupita cleared the kitchen table while her father got ready for his second job. Mr. Fuentes was of average height and thin. He wore a low side part similar to the late Cesar Chavez, a Mexican American labor leader. The two women had disappeared into the master bedroom. Lupita decided they were secretly viewing the latest of Quince Anos accessories that her mother had bought for Lupita's special day. Lupita knew it would be another nine months before she could see the precious treasures which would help usher in her coming-of-age celebration.

In the bedroom, the two women were indeed looking at the cute diamond chandelier earrings, studded tiara, bible and sparkling scepter that had been purchased courtesy of Pablo's part-time job at a tortilla factory.

"Are you sure Lupita won't try to take a peek?" questioned her aunt.

"You know Lupita is an obedient child." "She doesn't want to disappoint me or her dad." The women agreed and shoved the wooden chest back into the closet. "She also loves the daylight out of surprises," laughed Lupita's mom.

Downsizing, reduction in force. Lupita had no idea what these words meant. She had to find out though because ten minutes earlier she had heard her parents using them as they whispered in the hallway on the way to their room. Her papa had entered the house smelling of fresh tortillas and sat his hat down on the coffee table. He was not smiling his usual smile. Lupita and her mom picked up on it right away. They both stayed quiet and awaited his next action. Soon he spoke to Lupita and then took his wife's small hand and headed down the hall. That's when Lupita heard the words, "reduction in force." She could tell by the way her papa used them that they were significant.

Tia Gabriela was resourceful, she knew a lot of things and had good research skills. Lupita dialed her number and counted three rings. She hoped she would not have to leave a voice mail.

Her Uncle Eloy answered on the 4th ring. "Ola." He greeted his niece in his native tongue.

"Ola," she responded. Then she listened to her uncle; her other godparent, as he updated her on his latest invention idea. As he described the device, she tried to picture what it looked like and how it could be used.

As was typical, he used very few words, sometimes speaking in Spanish, sometimes in English. He paused often to ask, "Comprendes tu?" He wanted to make sure Lupita understood.

"Si Tio," she said periodically. Soon, she was able to explain her reason for calling.

"No, Tia G isn't here right now." "But I'll tell her you called." He seemed eager to get back to his invention. Lupita ended the call before she realized that she didn't have her aunt's cell phone number. She was too embarrassed to call back. She knew that if her mother was not behind closed doors, she could get it from her. She had to skip to plan B.

Plan B was to use a dictionary. Lupita went to the shelf and saw the volume was missing like a tooth that had fallen out of a child's mouth. She ran her wide fingers along the other shelves to see if it had been placed in the wrong spot. She stopped when the phone rang.

She jogged toward the phone, hoping it was her Tia Gabriela. Instead it was a call for her papa. She drug herself back to the shelves and scanned as high as she could reach. She then went into the garage for the ladder to help her search the higher shelves.

Later, she slowly descended the ladder empty-handed. When she brightened with another idea, she climbed down a little faster. She decided to use the Internet to find her elusive definitions. But her father was still on the phone, so she nixed that idea.

She scribbled a note to her parents, donned her favorite pink sweater and locked the door behind her.

At her best friend's house down the street, she was greeted by a solemn Ms. Diaz. "Lucia, Lupita is here," Ms. Diaz announced while escorting Lupita to the colorful living room.

Lucia, whose name meant "light", slowly entered the room and sat down next to Lupita. Her eyes were red-rimmed. She soon pulled a tissue out of the sleeve of her dress.

"Sorry, but I'm not living up to my name right now, I'm not the best of company today." She apologized and blew her nose.

Soon she continued. "My dad had an RIF at work," she announced. Lupita stopped her for an explanation. "Oh, sorry, it means a reduction in force." "In other words my dad just got cut from his job."

Lucia never finished her explanation. Lupita had sprang from the couch like a jack-in-the-box and bolted for the door. Now she understood. Her dad, her own dad had lost his evening job. The job that he had gotten to pay for Lupita's surgery and Fiesta Rosa expenses. That's what caused the whispers and closed doors in her otherwise open and lively home.

As Lupita walked home to what she called THE GOOD HOUSE, she lamented that she might have to spend the rest of her life as a fat girl. As she approached her Dallas home, located in the heart of Oak Cliff near Jefferson Boulevard, she considered that she at least had the good fortune to live in a tight-knit community with many Latino families that knew her family nearby. Many would be invited to her Quince Anos.

She also clarified that she didn't want to be rail thin, or grace runways as a top model. She just yearned to be more streamlined, thinner. She kicked rocks dotting the sidewalk. With each step she came to the slow realization that her parents were just as troubled as she was. She didn't need to go home and have a pity party. For those few minutes, she also remembered that her middle name, Suelo meant "consolation." She decided that her role would be to be a bright spot in her parent's day. As she turned her key in the lock, she made a silent pinky promise to herself to be a source of consolation to them.

How she would do it, she didn't yet know.

Lupita washed her hands and went to the refrigerator. Ever conscious that she was staring at the contents while letting cold air out, she made up her mind and removed the items that she needed. Then she got a paper bag from the countertop and removed an avocado that had ripened for a week with the help of an apple. The avocado yielded to the pressure of her thumb, but it wasn't mushy. She peeled it, mashed it and then squeezed lemon juice into it. She then added plain yogurt in place of sour cream and cocktail sauce into the bowl. Next, she included peeled, cooked, shredded shrimp. Soon, her signature guacamole was ready. She put it in the refrigerator and took the other avocado out of the bag to began making avocado cream with it. She put the apple in the refrigerator for an after-dinner snack.

While the chopped vegetables simmered in broth, she put on a CD of her parents' favorite romanzas.

With music in the air and pleasant smells wafting throughout THE GOOD HOUSE, Lupita's parents broke their spell of silence and emerged from the room holding hands.

"Lupita, you've done a marvelous job," her papa exclaimed. He rolled his rs as he spoke. Pretty soon the family was seated around the table enjoying the sumptuous feast lovingly prepared by Lupita.

It wasn't long before all of the Quesadillas with avocado cream, and guacamole with shrimp dip was all gone. After her meal Lupita enjoyed her favorite orange soda and then ate her apple.

"Lupita, we have some sad news for you." Her father told about his layoff.

Lupita smiled, "Yes, but you still have your full-time day job, right?" she asked.

Her papa brightened and nodded. "But I still don't think you understand," he said softly. He took her left hand and held it. "Meja, there's no money coming for us to pay our portion for the surgery." "With papa's last check we will buy your ceremony pillows, guest book, and the champagne glasses for your brindis." "We must, we just have to cancel the surgery."

"Okay papa," she replied. She knew the upcoming celebration would recognize her transition from childhood to maturity. She decided that she'd start the journey right away. "I can do without the medal and the high heel shoes of spun glass – and we can make the cake and perhaps sew the dresses." "As long as I have my family and friends, I'll be happy."

"Really baby?" her papa asked. He looked at his wife, and then they both looked at Lupita.

"Yes, papa, that's all it will take to make me truly glad."

Later that evening, they watched the news. The Dallas City Council was asking people to participate in a poll to rename Industrial Boulevard. Mr Fuentes wrote down the phone number given. The news anchor specified that it was one vote per person, three votes per phone number. The three of them called, and each selected Cesar Chavez, a family hero. Mr Fuentes called his sister and suggested that she and her husband do the same.

When Tia Gabriela visited on the following Saturday, she struck a pose just inside the doorway so everyone could see her plantain-colored skirt set. "What do you think of my kick pleats, hijo," she teasingly asked her older brother. Then she sashayed to the living room.

"It reminds me of you when you were sweet 16," he responded. Lupita smiled, watched and listened. This new information meant that her favorite aunt had not had a weight problem as a teenager. Lupita filed this detail away to explore at a later time. Lupita spoke up, "Tia, do you think Dallas will have a street named after Cesar Chavez?"

Her aunt responded that she did. "However, I think it might end up being Jefferson Boulevard around the corner from here, or Ross Avenue." "You know they have a School off of Ross Avenue which is named after him?"

"Yes, there are a few schools named after him, and his image is even on postage stamps," Lupita replied.

Soon the three females were centered around the dining tables looking at dress patterns and fabric swatches. It looked like her mother would be sewing all of the dresses to save money. "I like this one," Lupita finally announced. She pointed to a dress which was elegant but simple.

Lupita's mom was confident that she could make the dress. They started looking at the fabric.

"Green, I want a shade of green," Lupita stated confidently. "I want my theme to come from THE WIZARD OF OZ'S Emerald City." After hearing this, the women moved all other colors aside. Lupita eyed the various shades of green. They ranged from sea moss green, an iridescent green to a shade that reminded her of cucumbers. She decided on iridescent chartreuse because she had never seen anyone in a dress of that color.

While her tia returned to the store to buy enough fabric for Lupita's dress, Lupita's mother took her measurements. Her father came in from mowing the lawn and was relieved to see that the progress for Lupita's big day was continuing. He stopped and eyed the pattern.

"Papa doesn't want his Lupita in a sleeveless gown without a jacket," he stated firmly.

"No problem, papa." Lupita showed him the pattern for the bolero jacket that she would wear over her dress.

"Short and sweet – like my Lupita," he said while looking at the jacket picture. He kissed his daughter's jaw. "With the jacket, papa will be happy." He remembered something Lupita had said the previous week. "Yes, papa will be truly glad."

Lupita and her mother removed the pattern pieces and Lupita cut them out while her mother made dinner. It reminded her of the time she'd cut shaped fabric pieces when her grandmother taught her how to make a quilt. When Pablo Fuentes thought about how well Lupita had accepted the news of his job loss and found an alternative to a store-bought dress, he felt lifted and comforted. He had not failed his Lupita after all. He had given her an opportunity to show what she was made of. And she was made of good Fuentes stock with a bounty of determination and drive. He would soon see just how far those two qualities would take her.

"Why Lupita, you've never even spent one night away from home, away from us." "To stay with your padrinos for eight weeks!" "Eight weeks," he repeated.

Lupita sat quietly. Her mother was doing the same. Soon her mother gave her a smile, which encouraged her to speak up. It reminded Lupita of her aunt's twinkling eyes. "Your Lupita is growing up, papa," she announced. "I'll learn about portion control and have a daily walking companion in Tia G." "This is like the surgery's replacement or substitute."

"Madre de Dios." "First I lose my job, then I lose my daughter." Mr. Fuentes ran his hand through his wavy hair and looked at his wife.

Maria Fuentes sat fingering the fabric, which would be used to make Lupita's dress. In her mind's eye, she saw herself having enough extra fabric to sew a tie and kerchief for her husband, and a sash for herself. She felt confident that Lupita would reach her goal.

On the other hand, the wheels of Pablo Fuentes' mind were whirling. Seeing the fabric reminded him that the idea to have his wife sew the dresses had been Lupita's. He realized that spending eight weeks away from home was yet another solution that Lupita had ferreted out. With that in mind, he weakened his resolve.

"Do you think you can lose that much weight in eight weeks and stay on target to lose more after learning Tia's regimen?" he asked.

"I can do it papa." "Tia G is my sponsor for the Quince Anos, she wants to help me with the temporary and the permanent answers that I need." She leaned against her papa and continued. "It's not just for my Quince Anos, it's for my health and for my life." "Por me vida," she repeated the last three words in Spanish.

Pablo Fuentes ran his hand through his hair again. He looked at his wife, who smiled and nodded. "What you need to do is become a lawyer because you know how to present a good argument." He smiled and opened his arms for Lupita. "What can I say, but 'yes' to such a good idea." "I'm glad, you're glad." "Yes, everybody's felicitous" "You can go to Gabriela and Eloy's for eight weeks – but not a minute longer." "Mama and papa will miss you, THE GOOD HOUSE will miss you." "Go! Leave soon before I change my mind."

Lupita loosened herself from her papa's hug and ran to pack. She phoned Lucia and then Tia G with the news.

Her papa would find out the next day how fortunate it was that they had made arrangements for Lupita to be away for a while. His generous boss had a surprise for him when he arrived at work the next day.

Lupita was using Tia Gabriela's cell phone, which she now kept with her all the time. Her parents insisted that they have a way to stay in touch. She tucked the phone back in its case and clipped it to the top of her jogging pants. She and Tia Gabriela were about to power walk on the soft turf at a college near Tia G's house.

After a few minutes of silent walking, Tia G spoke. "Okay, you've got a good stride and pace," she complimented. "Now start swinging your arms like this." She demonstrated and they resumed their walk with all arms swinging. After about 15 minutes, they stopped for water.

"One more time?" Tia G asked. Lupita agreed and they started around the track again. Lupita recalled two weeks earlier when she could only make it around once, after which she was often huffing and puffing on the way to the car. She also remembered how sore her muscles had been.

Today after the second time around the track, Lupita listened to her calm, even breathing. No huffs, no puffs. Two weeks had produced some results.

Later, back at Tia G's house, the two nibbled on green grapes and chatted. In Tia G's house, they never ate while watching TV. Her tia had told her that people tended to eat a lot more when watching TV. Lupita knew she'd have to break this old habit. Tia referred to it as a lifestyle change.

The two ate an early dinner of steamed carrots, salad, and baked chicken. Then Lupita did her homework. It was her first assignment for the new school year.

When the house phone rang later, it was Tio Eloy calling to report that he had advanced to the final stage of an invention competition in Las Vegas. He had prepared a prototype, or model of his invention and Lupita had helped him write a short presentation to give to the judges.

"Eloy might win prize money to mass produce his device," Tia G told her after hanging up. She was proud of her husband, who was a mechanic by trade.

Lupita finished her homework and then called the members of her court to tell them what she had discovered about eating while watching TV. Then she and her aunt chopped vegetables and made purees and juices using a food processor.

After a nice, relaxing shower, Lupita got on the scale in the bathroom. She realized that they might have to buy a smaller pattern for her dress. Before bedtime, Lupita read a small section of the Dallas Morning News, which stated that Industrial Boulevard would be renamed Riverfront Boulevard. It further stated that the Dallas City Council would recommend that Ross Avenue be renamed for Cesar Chavez.

Lucia's dress was the first one finished by Ms Fuentes. Lucia called Lupita while still at THE GOOD HOUSE before returning home with her pea green dress. She reported her immense satisfaction with her dress. Lupita invited her over to spend the night. Her tia had given her permission to invite her friends over for a slumber party. Still in line for their dresses were Adela, Nilda, Eve, and Ida. They were holding their breaths in anticipation of seeing their finished gowns in various shades of green. Ms Fuentes was sewing the dresses in rank order according to how long each girl had been friends with her daughter.

Lupita and the girls were up after 3:00am and showed no signs of weariness. They had embroidered, stuffed, and sewn Lupita's ceremony pillow. It now sat on the dresser in a clear plastic bag.

Now they were discussing a homework assignment. They had to do a report which revealed information about themselves that most of the class did not already know. It was due on Monday. Each student would be called upon to present their reports with props during the following week. Eva was going to share that she had mixed heritage. Her mother was Hispanic, and her father was a medium-skinned black man, who looked a bit like Presidential hopeful, Barack Obama. Ida and Nilda had not yet decided what to do their reports about and Edela and Lucia were doing a report and demonstration that centered around their mariachi experience. Both girls were accomplished mariachi singers and dancers. "I'll wear my skirt of bold hues and Edela will wear her flouncy pastel skirt," Lucia announced. "Perhaps my dad can come and play his guitarrAn." "He's not working right now."

"What are you going to do?" Adela asked Lupita. Lupita explained that she would do a presentation about measuring meal portions and exercizing for weight loss.

Quiet, soft-spoken Ida finally spoke up. "People are asking if Lupita is sick because her clothes are a little baggy." "I wasn't going to say anything at first."

"I know," added Eva. "They accuse her of sagging on purpose when she wears pants."

"I don't concern myself about what people think, as long as they are not doing any-thing to hurt me," Lupita announced. Soon everyone got quieter and started getting prepared for a few hours of sleep. Before Lupita went to sleep, she crossed herself and smiled a smile of contentment.

On Monday at school, the class watched as Adela and Lucia performed their energetic routine with skirts swooshing and swirling around the room. Lucia's dad played a large Mexican guitar and his brother played a vihuela, a small round-backed guitar. A CD of violins accompanied in the background. Then Adela told a little bit about the Aztec culture, which influenced mariachi song, dance, and music. As soon as Adela sat down, Lupita got up with her measuring cup, bottled water and other props. Their teacher, Ms. Herndon, had told her she would be next.

She sat her props on a desk and began. "I'm on a journey to health and wellness." "My goal is to lose 40 pounds within a year, cut back on sugar, and change my lifestyle," she began. She explained how Diabetes ran in her family, robbing one grandmother of a limb, and a grandfather of his eyesight. She showed them how she now poured a cup of cereal in a measuring cup, as opposed to dumping a bowlful directly into her cereal bowl. "Once I've added milk, I put the cereal box away." She shared how she used to eat a few bowls full on Saturdays while watching cartoons. She joked about how it would leave her so stuffed that she had to take a mid-morning siesta.

She noticed some students got out paper and pencils and started taking notes. Soon Lupita was marching around the room, demonstrating the power walk.

Four weeks later, her parents phoned from Culebra, an island off the coast of Puerto Rico. Her dad's boss had given them a two week all-expense paid trip in recognition of his 8 years of loyal service. Mr. Fuentes and his wife took turns chatting with Lupita while walking the sands of Playa Zoni Beach.

"I've lost 17 pounds," Lupita announced. She assured her parents that she and her tia were using sunscreen and drinking lots of water. "Are you using sunscreen?" she returned the question. Soon Lupita was handing off the phone to her aunt.

Lupita stopped to tie a shoelace and then jogged to catch up with her aunt.

"They will he home in 3 days," stated Tia G. She told Lupita that they would be picking them up from the airport and then having them over for dinner. While they walked, they discussed menu ideas for that welcome home dinner.

That night, Lupita slept more peacefully and sweetly than she had in years. She knew that her sleep problems had began when she started to add a lot of extra weight at age 12. She concluded that the extra weight and insomia were somehow connected.

It was easy to tell that her parents were teasing when they pretended they didn't see her and her aunt standing beyond the jet gate, a pathway connecting the plane to the airport. First they walked right past them, then they boomeranged back and pretended to be still searching for their loved ones. Lupita and her aunt played along.

"You two look like members of the jet-set," Maria Fuentes gushed. She had learned the word while on vacation. Lupita and her tia were both wearing linen skirt suits the color of honeydew melons. Lupita wore a bangle bracelet and had on her first pair of pierced earrings. Her parents had given her permission to pierce her ears over the phone. Her dad called her a dish of lime sherbert with chocolate and caramel syrup on top.

Her parents competed for her attention. They lavished praise on her before turning to greet Gabriela.

While Lupita's father walked with his sister, Lupita and her mama walked behind them. Lupita announced that she had lost 3 more pounds. Her mother was proud as a peacock.

Dinner consisted of Spinach Empanadas, salad with lemon zest, squash casserole and baked fish. Lupita put salad dressing on the table for her parents, but when they saw her enjoy her salad without it, they followed suit. Lupita's mom reported that she would be ready to start on Adela's cucumber and lime shaded dress the next day. Nilda's dress would be next with its solid lime green fabric. Then would come Eve and Ida's, one in green and silver and the other in green and gold. The one thing that all girls shared in common were the trumpet sleeves, which are sleeves that fit from the shoulder to the elbow and then flare out into a bell shape.

A couple of weeks later, Lupita, Eve, Ida and Adela went to the mall with Tia G to get a complimentary beauty hour at one of the cosmetic counters. Tia G had parked a good distance away and they had a long walk while they talked about their day. Eve said she had been awakened at dawn by her mother to help make tamales from scratch. Earlier at Tia G's house, the girls, along with Lucia, had sat amongst green fabric remnants and cotton stuffing. Together they made a small quilt for Lupita. Lucia had returned home with it and was planning to add a secret touch before taking it to Lupita's house.

At the make-up counter, they received make-up tips and then had their faces made up. Special cards were used to record which products and shades were used on each girl. Lupita received a kit with sample products, since she was the one planning her Quince Anos. She ended up with a fresh-faced rosy look, a sharp contrast to Eva who had shades of dark caramel that highlighted her mixed ethnicity.

The other girls had shades of light brown. Everyone's eyebrows were defined with hues that matched their hair color.

In lieu of going to the food court, they went to a nearby park and enjoyed the picnic lunch that Lupita had prepared. Lupita had brought along colored markers and paper plates and cups. She placed them around the redwood picnic table and the girls put their names on them while Lupita took out the food. The last stop was Lupita's house. Eve went inside and tried on her dress and took it home with exceeding joy.

Lupita hugged her aunt. "3 months left and I am a new girl – thanks to you." She waved when her aunt drove away, and then took her suitcases to her room. While she was unpacking, her mother entered the room and sat by her.

"Welcome home, meja." "Mama, papa and THE GOOD HOUSE missed you so much." Her mother said she loved the make-up and was certain that papa would approve.

When Lupita had exactly one month left, her total weight loss equaled 30 pounds. During the past 10 days, she had not dropped any weight, even though she was doing the same things as before. But she was content and felt better than ever before in her life. People called and encouraged her. She always shared some new discovery and admonished them to try it.

After speaking to Adela, she went down the hall and knocked on her parents' door. When given permission to enter, she told her mama that she was ready for her final measurements. Afterwards, she knew work on her dress would begin in earnest.

Lupita was satisfied with her new measurements. She could tell that she had lost inches by the way her clothes sagged on her frame. Her mother told her that if she lost more weight before the celebration, she could always make adjustments. Later, Lupita made breakfast and then ate in solitude while reading a book. She went walking after leaving her parents a note.

While walking, she thought about the letter that she would hand out a few days before Valentine's Day. She wanted people to bring her small pieces of fruit instead of chocolate or other sweets. Satisfied that she would get the cooperation of her teacher and most classmates, she turned her attention to the dress that her mother would make for her. She made a decision to stay out of the room while her mother sewed. She would not view her dress until the day of the event. She wanted to be astonished by her mother's accomplishment.

It wasn't as easy as she thought. Sometimes she wanted to take a peek at the work in progress. A lover of that feeling of wonder and suspense, she decided not to deprive herself of the upcoming joyous surprise. So she waited and she wondered and she waited some more.

On Valentine's Day, a few people gave everyone suckers or chocolate during the party. Lupita politely thanked them and put the sweets in her backpack. One-by-one, her classmates filed by her desk with cards and clusters of grapes, an apple, an orange, or another healthy snack. Lupita sat with her leg up, having injured her ankle while jogging. A few of the girls gave her hair accessories, which she put in her hair right away. It didn't matter to her whether they matched her persimmon dress or not. Her brown waves were soon dotted with colorful hues.

It warmed her heart the way some classmates shared that they had adopted a new lifestyle change. "I drink my water an hour before or an hour after meals," a red-haired girl named Delores told her. The previous year, despite a remarkable performance at cheerleader tryouts, Delores had been eliminated. Rumor had it that her excess weight was the dealbreaker, or reason she lost. Delores was on a mission to lose 20 pounds and try out again the following year.

Her trilingual friend, Daya, told her that she had become a vegetarian, because to her that was a lifestyle change that could produce the results she wanted. Daya's father worked at the shipping company with Lupita's dad.

Even rail-thin Lucia told her that her family had stopped watching TV while eating. "We talk instead, and are getting to know one another better," Lucia reported.

Bobby Fentwood, the class clown, walked behind Lupita and draped a rubber snake around her neck. When Lupita awarded him with a squeal, he ran off into a corner and laughed.

Ms Fuentes had brought in a tray of baby carrots, celery, and ranch dip as an alternate choice for the celebrants. Hidden in the trunk of her car was Ida's completed dress. Lupita knew it would be a pleasant surprise for her newest friend. They had got to know each other the previous year during a fire drill. Although they lived quite far apart, they kept their friendship active through regular phone calls and occasional outings with just the two of them.

An only child like Lupita, Ida let out a high-pitched squeal when she saw her vision of lovliness after school let out. When Ms Fuentes gave her a ride home, both girls sat in the back. "I'm back to being a chauffer," joked Ms. Fuentes, who was used to these two girls wanting to maximize drive time by sitting together. While they were riding, Ida handed Lupita a red envelope. Inside was a lovely valentine card from Bobby Fentwood. "He likes you Lupita, that's why he always teases you," Ida reported. Lupita blushed, but did not respond.

Preparing a shopping list for the upcoming week proved a little more challenging than usual. Lupita and her mom planned the week's menu, including Lupita's Quince Anos ingredients. Topping the shopping list were radishes, carrots, cucumbers, tomatoes, honeydew melons, plums, peaches, and green apples. These were items that they all liked and they expected to reap a bounteous harvest of good health by eating more of these and other fruits and vegetables.

What made the list more complicated was the substitution of low fat and low calorie ingredients. For instance, they were buying 8 ounces of low-fat cheese, instead of block cheese for the beef enchiladas. In place of oil would be low-calorie cooking spray. Lastly, they had to purchase the leanest can of chili available at the market.

Lupita got up and looked into the pantry. "We have chili powder, but no cumin," she announced. Her mother added cumin to the list. She also wrote down corn tortillas, onions, and enchilada sauce, after Lupita reported that there wasn't any of those items in the refrigerator or pantry. Ms Fuentes planned to make enough enchiladas to have a few days of leftovers so that she could concentrate on finishing Lupita's dress.

The last item she wrote down was postage stamps, so they could mail Lupita's Quince Anos invitations. Lupita and her mother agreed that if they couldn't get stamps featuring the icon, Cesar Chavez, they would go to the post office to purchase them.

When they got to the grocery store, to their delight, the supermercado did indeed sell stamps featuring the leader of the United Farm Workers. The reason this choice was important to them is that both sets of Lupita's grandparents had been migrant farm workers. They had told Lupita of their many days of hardship and terrible working conditions, which improved when Chavez began to agitate for change in the 1960's.

Lupita's dress did indeed require some adjustments. Her mother had taken the last measurements the night before the Quincenera. She added pleats in the waistline and narrowed the sleeves of the bolero jacket.

Lupita and her court were back at the mall for their final make-up session. Each lady pulled out the file cards prepared during the previous visit and worked to re-create the look they had created weeks before. Lucia went with the same shades as Lupita, since they were similar in coloring. Earlier that morning, they had visited a beauty college to have their hair fixed. At both places, Tia G – resplendent in a retro print dress of bubble gum purple, eggshell and pastel pink – had walked from station to station offering tips as she checked on each girls' progress.

Lupita was the last one finished. "You look like a doll," her aunt said. Lupita blushed beneath the light make-up. She donned plum eyeshadow and a mauve shade of lipstick. Her blush was slightly bolder, and made her olive cheeks look dew-kissed.

As they trekked across the parking lot to the car, the girls chatted about their busy day, which had started with a wake-up call from Tia G at 7:00am.

"I'm not a morning person," stated Lucia. She brightened and added, "The only person I'd get up early like this for is Lupita." The other girls agreed. Lucia explained that her family was surviving off of her father's unemployment checks and he earned extra cash by mowing lawns in the neighborhood. She reported that he was scheduled to audition for a local mariachi band. If chosen, he would earn $100 for doing two gigs per week.

When they finally reached the car, Lupita pulled her bottled water out of the cupholder where she'd left it. Between sips she read the to-do list for each girl. One by one, Tia G dropped off her charges with instructions on when to arrive at the Fuentes' home.

At home, Tia G's husband and a host of other aunts and uncles were finishing up batches of low calorie guacamole dip, mango salsa, tortilla soup and chicken fajitas. One aunt had been up all night making the tortillas from scratch. The lemon chiffon cake cooled on the counter awaiting Tia G's decorative touch.

While Lupita soaked in a lavender and vanilla scented bubble bath – her dad finished sewing baby pearls onto her dress. He carefully counted each one to make sure he added the correct quantity. A few tears flowed down his cheek as he traveled down memory lane. He recalled bringing Lupita home from the hospital and carrying her on a pillow for fear of hurting her. He remembered other milestones and birthdays. Lupita staggering around in her pink play heels with large rhinestones that he had bought her at the five and dime. Mr Fuentes had to admit that he was proud of the way she had developed over the last year. Today – she could be declared a young lady as far as he was concerned. He counted off wisdom, resourcefulness, compassion and other qualities that he had seen emerge in her lately. Had she complained about having to scale down the Quincenera celebration, cancel the surgery and move the celebration from the banquet hall to THE GOOD HOUSE? No,instead she had found alternative solutions. His Lupita had started a journey without and within.

He recalled how often she spent time educating family and friends about healthy lifestyles. As she'd learned, she'd taught. Many loved ones were making changes in their own patterns because of Lupita. Today's menu had been her idea.

From down the hall, Lupita heard strains of music from THE WIZARD OF OZ playing. She knew it was time to get out of the tub and get ready. Besides, she didn't want to shrivel up like a raisin in the sun. Her mother soon came into the room and helped her put on her hose and polished her nails. After Lupita's nails dried, her mother brought out the long-awaited dress. Lupita drew in her breath. Her dress was more beautiful than her heart could have ever wished. Soon her Damas came into the room and "oohed' and "aahed" over the dress. Next, fresh flowers from the Diaz' garden were pinned in her hair. Her mother removed the Bobby pins which had formed tight pincurls from Lupita's hair, and the brownish curls cascaded down her shoulders and back.

When strains of SOMEWHERE OVER THE RAINBOW began to waft through the house and yard, Lupita knew that she and her friends could no longer stay holed up in her room. The Court preceded her out of the room. Alone again, Lupita took one look around the blue bedroom. How many more years she'd be there she didn't know. What she did know was that she'd like to re-decorate it soon. Out with the girlish look and on to something more mature. Soon her mama knocked on the door. It was time for Lupita to proceed to her waiting loved ones. As Lupita walked down the hallway on her papa's arm, Tia G viewed her over a champagne glass. Those wondrous brown eyes twinkling over the glass gave Lupita confidence. She locked eyes with her tia and smiled a big Kool-aid grin. Before long she could see the table with extensions spread out with a marvelous centerpiece, and other delightful surprises.

Lupita wished she had practiced walking in heels. In a few moments, she'd trade her flat shoes for some grown-up ones. Sure, a few years back she used to play dress-up with her mother's high heels. She would parade around the house and model for her audience of two. But it had been many years ago since she'd done that. She paraded down the hall escorted by her father. Once she entered the room, her papa bent down and slid her flat shoes off. In their place, he put on her peep toe shoes. They were a symbol of her maturity. When her father was finished, Lupita's cousin Mario serenaded her with song.

Tia G stepped forward and handed Lupita her LAST DOLL. A little chubby, the doll had dark wavy hair like Lupita and wore a dress made from the same fabric as Lupita's. Lupita had no idea that her mother had secretly made that dress. She was only aware of the tie, kerchief, and sash that her mother had made. Her papa proudly wore his items as expected, but her mama was wearing her sash as a scarf around her slender neck. Lupita wondered why.

After thanking her Tia G., Lupita handed her doll to Lucia – who was standing by her like a sentry.

It was time for Lupita to start the waltz. Everyone cleared the floor so she could dance with her papa. Lupita put her head on her papa's shoulder and listened to him speak while they danced. "My Lupita knows how to find treasure in stones and make-do with very little." "When life hands her lemons – she makes lemonade." Lupita raised her head briefly to look into her papa's moist eyes. Her papa began to whisper again.

"Do you know that each little pearl on your dress stands for some special quality that papa saw in you this past year?" Lupita said she hadn't known that. "There's a total of 30, sewn by papa's loving hands." During your brindis I will tell you what each pearl stands for." He turned her around so she could see her mother. "In 6 months you will have a little sister or brother – can you see?" Lupita smiled at her mama, who winked at her and then rubbed her bumpy belly. Now Lupita understood why her mama could not wear the sash around her middle.

He turned her to look the other way. She could see glitter stars arched over the table, marblelized place cards for each guest, and green frosted take-out boxes with colored tissues. Later she'd find out those bags were chock full of almonds, bags of craisins, raisins, and other healthy snacks. Each guests would go home with a box at night's end. These were all things that were not even in her original Quincinera plans! It was almost more that her young heart could hold. She bubbled over with gratitude.

At the arranged signal others got on the dance floor, starting with Lupita's court. As Lupita danced the night away, her eyes danced in equal merriment. When some guests stepped up their routine and leaped during The Electric Slide, Lupita's heart leaped with them. When her father spoke affirming words during the brindis, the words forged a direct pathway from her ears to her young, tender heart. Between the Latino dances of expression, like the Macarena and the Salsa, the love of people around her, and the words spoken by her papa, Lupita's self-esteem was cemented that day. She was awash with joy and overflowing with gladness!

Author bio

Shirley A. Franklin is a Reading teacher in the Dallas area. The mother of one son, she has been writing and inspiring others to do so for many years. Many of her works are a tribute to two hard-working parents, who nurtured and fueled her desire to write from the early days of her youth.